DATE DUE

A GROWING-UP BOOK™

That Makes Me Angry!

By Anthony Best
Illustrated by Tom Cooke

A GOLDEN BOOK • NEW YORK
Published by Golden Books Publishing Company, Inc., in cooperation
with Children's Television Workshop

One morning Ernie looked out the window and wondered what to do that day. Bert was settled into a chair with his new book, *Famous Pigeons*.

Ernie watched some leaves and bits of paper dancing and swirling along Sesame Street. "Bert," he said suddenly. "Guess what?" Then instead of letting Bert guess, he told him. "It's windy, Bert! It's a good day to go to the park and fly a kite!"

"That's nice, Ernie," said Bert. He was enjoying his book.

But Ernie leaned over the top of *Famous Pigeons* and said, "I'll go buy a kite, Bert, and you fix a picnic lunch for us. Okay, Bert?"

It wasn't okay with Bert, not at first. He wasn't fond of picnics on windy days. He was happy sitting and reading. But he began to think what fun it would be to watch a kite swoop and glide high in the air while he and Ernie held on tightly to the string and munched sandwiches and apples.

"Well…" he said at last. "Okay, Ernie."

"Swell, Bert," said Ernie. "Meet me at the big statue in the park with our lunch."

"All right, Ernie. The big statue is—" Bert was going to say "fine," but Ernie had already slammed the door and was on his way.

Ernie chose an orange kite at the toy store and ran with it to the park.

He sat down under the big statue of a boy and a girl on a horse and began to put the kite together. "Bert will love this kite," he said to himself. "Orange is his favorite color."

Meanwhile, Bert made two peanut-butter-and-banana sandwiches, Ernie's favorite. He put them in his lunch box with two apples and two cartons of milk, and set off to meet Ernie in the park.

He sat down under the big statue of Mother Goose. "I hope Ernie gets here soon with the kite," he thought.

But Ernie didn't get there soon. He was sitting beside the big statue of a boy and a girl on a horse, waiting for Bert.

"Where is my old buddy Bert?" he wondered. "He should have been here by now."

Before long Bert was wondering the same thing
about Ernie.

"Where can that Ernie be?" he thought. "He really
should have been here by now."

Ernie waited and waited. He was getting restless.
"I wish Bert would hurry," he said. "We're wasting all
the wind!"

It seemed to Bert that he had been waiting for hours. "This is ridiculous," he said. "I could have been sitting at home all this time, reading my new book."

Suddenly Ernie remembered that he had left Bert happily reading *Famous Pigeons*. "I'll bet I know what happened to Bert," he said. "He is reading his silly book and has forgotten all about our picnic and flying a kite with me! Oh, that makes me angry!"

By now, Bert had an idea about what had become
of Ernie. "This is just like Ernie!" he said. "He found
something else to do and forgot all about buying a kite.
He probably met Prairie Dawn and went off to play
catch or jacks. That really makes me angry!"

So Ernie and Bert gave up waiting for each other and trudged home.

Bert got home first. He shoved the lunch box into the refrigerator and plopped down in his chair with *Famous Pigeons*. Before he could turn one page, the door flew open and there was Ernie.

"I'm very angry with you, Bert!" yelled Ernie.
"I'm very angry with you, Ernie!" yelled Bert.
Ernie and Bert stared at each other.
"Why are *you* angry with *me*?" Bert asked, amazed.
"Because you forgot all about having a picnic lunch
and flying a kite with me, that's why!" answered Ernie.

"But that's why I'm angry with you!" said Bert. Then Bert ran to the refrigerator and got the lunch box to show Ernie. Ernie pulled the kite in the door to show Bert.

"See?" said Ernie. "I didn't forget. I got this kite in your favorite color and waited at the big statue of the horse."

"And I made your favorite sandwiches and waited at the big statue of Mother Goose," said Bert.

"Oops!" said Ernie. "We did forget something, Bert!"

"Right," said Bert. "We forgot there are *two* big statues in the park!"

And they both began to laugh. Then Bert looked out the window. "There's still time to fly a kite, Ernie," he said.

"Come on, Bert!" said Ernie. "Let's go!"

Back in the park, Ernie and Bert munched
sandwiches and apples while they held the string and
watched the kite swoop and glide high in the sky.
"See, Bert? Isn't this fun?" asked Ernie.
"Yes, Ernie. And we're not angry anymore."